BE MINE

BY BRENDA PONNAY

ISBN: 9781623953218 • eISBN:9781623953232
ePib ISBN: 9781623953225
Published in the United States
by Xist Publishing
www.xistpublishing.com

I'M NUTS
ABOUT YOU.

BE MINE!

YOU NEED A
BEAR HUG!

I BLUB YOU.

YOU'RE THE CAT'S PAJAMAS!

I'M CRAZY ABOUT YOU!

YOU MAKE ME CROW!

HEY CUTIE!

I'M FUZZY
ON THE INSIDE

I'M HEAD OVER HEELS
FOR YOU!

HEY CUPCAKE!

WHAT'S UP HONEY BUNNY?

OH, LOVE BUG!

I JUST WANNA
PINCH YOU!

HEY FOXY!

YOU SHOOT ME
TO THE MOON!

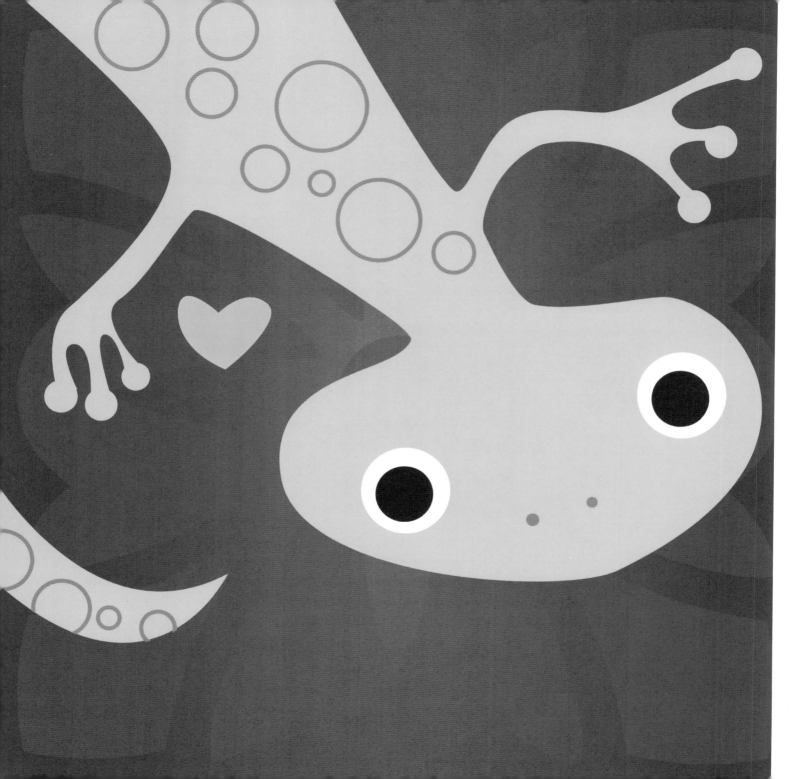

I'M STUCK ON YOU!

I LIKE YOU
WARTS AND ALL

WHOOOOOOOO
LOVES YOU?

Made in the USA
San Bernardino, CA
28 January 2013